How m

Fill in the boxes ~~...~~ these four friends are doing.

out of

are
singing

out of

are
sitting

How many candles?

Fill in the boxes to show the fraction of the candles that are lit.

out of

are lit

Thanks for the card!

Happy Birthday!

USBORNE KEY SKILLS

Practice Pad
Fractions

Written by

Simon Tudhope and Holly Bathie

Illustrated by Elisa Paganelli

Designed by Sharon Cooper
Series Editor: Felicity Brooks

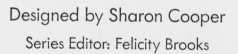

$$\frac{2}{3} + \frac{1}{3} = \frac{3}{3}$$

At the back of this pad you'll find the answer pages,
and also a fractions wall to help you with your calculations.

Painted shapes

Draw a line to connect each painted
shape to the correct fraction.

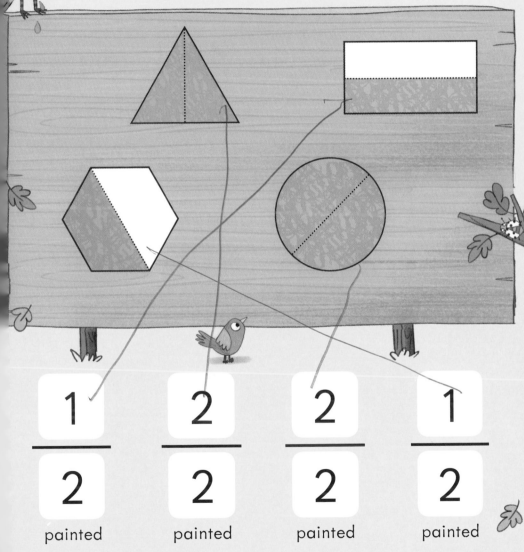

$$\frac{1}{2}$$ painted

$$\frac{2}{2}$$ painted

$$\frac{2}{2}$$ painted

$$\frac{1}{2}$$ painted

Painted shapes

4

Draw a line to connect each painted shape to the correct fraction.

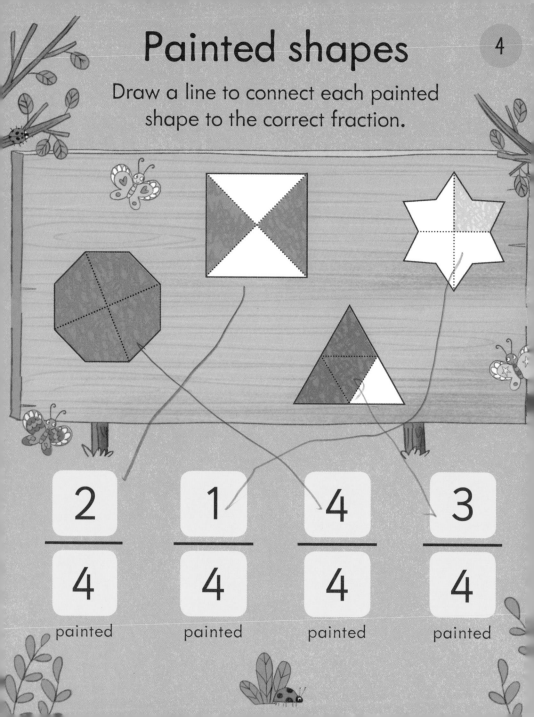

$$\frac{2}{4}$$
painted

$$\frac{1}{4}$$
painted

$$\frac{4}{4}$$
painted

$$\frac{3}{4}$$
painted

Painted shapes

Draw a line to connect each painted
shape to the correct fraction.

$$\frac{3}{4}$$ painted

$$\frac{1}{2}$$ painted

$$\frac{2}{4}$$ painted

$$\frac{1}{4}$$ painted

Dividing into halves

Zeb has divided his vegetable patch into halves.
Write the correct fraction inside each part.

Dividing into quarters

Zeb has divided his flowerbed into quarters.
Write the correct fraction inside each part.

Equal parts

The animals have divided their cakes
into two pieces. Circle the cake that
is divided into halves.

Equal parts

The animals have divided their cakes into four pieces. Circle the cake that is divided into quarters.

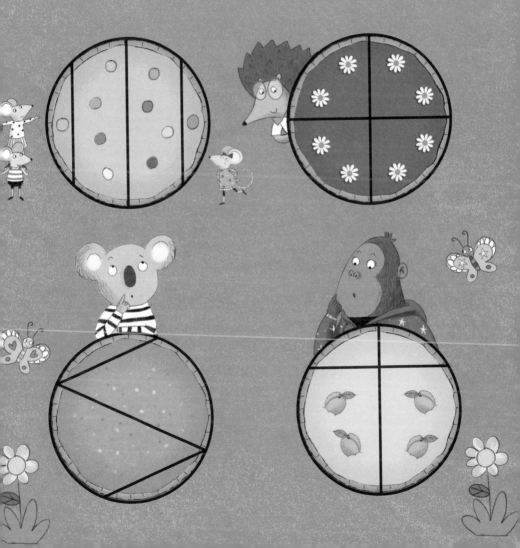

What fraction?

Look at the flower below. Then, fill in the boxes to show the fraction of the flower that has nibbles in it, and the fraction that does not.

$$\frac{}{4}$$

with nibbles

$$\frac{}{4}$$

no nibbles

Adding fractions

Wolfy and Ping each have half a pizza. They want to put their halves together on one plate. Complete the calculation to show how much pizza they will have altogether.

$$\frac{1}{2} + \frac{1}{2} = \frac{}{}$$ or

whole
pizza

Adding fractions

Bruce and Hop love the apple pie at the café. They each have one quarter of it. Complete the calculation to show the fraction of the pie they have altogether.

Are you daydreaming again, Hop?

$$\frac{1}{4} + \frac{1}{4} = \frac{}{}$$

Adding fractions

Gloria has decorated three quarters of her cake.
Decorate the other quarter for her, then complete
the calculation to show the fraction of
her cake that is decorated.

Careful, Pat!

$$\frac{3}{4} + \frac{}{} = \frac{}{} \text{ or } 1$$

whole
cake

Subtracting fractions

Kat cut her tomato into quarters. She has eaten three quarters. Complete the calculation to show the fraction of the tomato she has left.

1

whole tomato

or $\dfrac{4}{4} - \dfrac{3}{4} = $

Subtracting fractions

Zeb and Ping are sharing an egg sandwich. Zeb has eaten two quarters of it. Complete the calculation to show the fraction of the sandwich left for Ping.

$$1 \text{ or } \frac{4}{4} - \frac{2}{4} = \frac{}{}$$

whole sandwich

Subtracting fractions

Zeb, Pat and Kat have eaten half a lemon cake between them. Complete the calculation to show the fraction of cake that is left.

$$1 - \frac{1}{2} = \underline{\hspace{2cm}}$$

whole cake

What fraction?

Gloria has fruit for lunch. Fill in the blank boxes to show the fraction of her lunchbox that contains each fruit.

banana

grapes

strawberries

How many...?

Fill in the boxes to show the fraction
of the group doing each activity.

watering
plants

digging

How many flowers?

Pat has three flowers. Fill in the boxes to show the fraction of his flowers that are red.

red

Painted shapes

Draw a line to connect each painted
shape to the correct fraction.

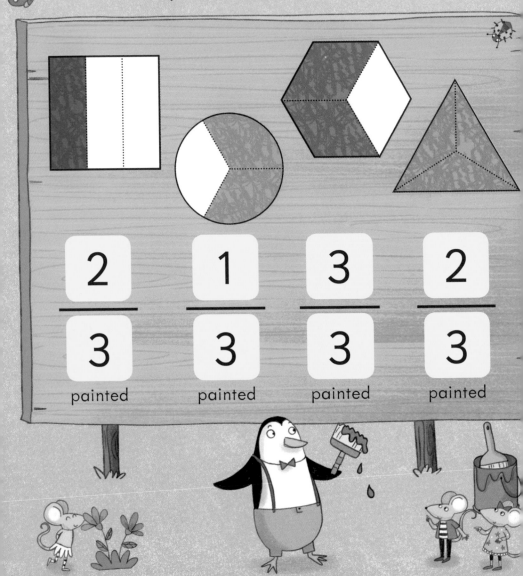

$\frac{2}{3}$ painted $\frac{1}{3}$ painted $\frac{3}{3}$ painted $\frac{2}{3}$ painted

Equal parts

The animals have divided their cakes into three pieces. Circle the cake that is divided into thirds.

What fraction?

Look at the flower below. Then, fill in the boxes to show the fraction of the flower that has nibbles in it, and the fraction that does not.

with nibbles   no nibbles

Adding fractions

One third of these penguins are wearing bow ties.
Draw a bow tie on another penguin, then complete
the calculation to show the fraction of
the group wearing bow ties.

$$\frac{}{} + \frac{}{} = \frac{}{}$$

Adding fractions

Zeb has placed two thirds of his lemon cake onto a plate and has another third to add. Complete the calculation to show the fraction of cake that will be on the plate.

It looks so tasty!

$$\frac{\quad}{\quad} + \frac{\quad}{\quad} = \frac{\quad}{\quad} \text{ or } 1$$

whole cake

Subtracting fractions

Wolfy is hungry today. He has eaten two thirds of the café's fish pie. Complete the calculation to show the fraction of pie that is left.

$$1 - \frac{}{} = \frac{}{}$$

whole
pie

Subtracting fractions

The mice have found two thirds of a fruit loaf. They will eat one of the thirds. Complete the calculation to show the fraction of fruit loaf that will be left.

$$\frac{2}{3} - \frac{}{} = \frac{}{}$$

How many...?

These friends are working on articles and pictures for their magazine. Fill in the boxes to show the fraction of the group doing each activity.

painting

writing

How many flags?

Fill in the boxes to show the fraction of the flags that have stripes.

Hey, wake up!

with stripes

Draw a line to connect each painted
shape to the correct fraction.

$$\frac{2}{5}$$ painted

$$\frac{1}{5}$$ painted

$$\frac{3}{5}$$ painted

$$\frac{4}{5}$$ painted

Dividing into fifths

Zeb has divided his flowerbed into fifths.
Write the correct fraction inside each part.

Equal parts

The mice have divided their blocks of cheese into five pieces. Circle the block of cheese that is divided into fifths.

Look at the flower below. Then, fill in the boxes to show the fraction of the flower that has nibbles in it, and the fraction that does not.

with nibbles

no nibbles

Adding fractions

Bruce has decorated two fifths of his brownie with dark chocolate and will decorate the rest with white chocolate. Complete the calculation to show the fraction of brownie that will be decorated with chocolate.

Nearly finished!

$$\frac{}{} + \frac{}{} = \frac{}{} \text{ or } 1$$

whole brownie

Adding fractions

Pin has one fifth of Zeb's birthday cake. Zeb has eaten too much and gives Pin his fifth, too. Complete the calculation to show the fraction of the cake Pin has altogether.

Hop has eaten two fifths of her mousse.
Complete the calculation to show
the fraction of mousse she has left.

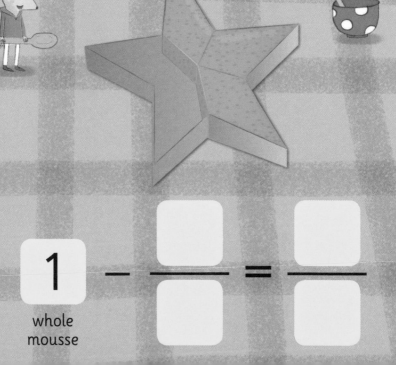

Would you
like some
too?

$$1 \text{ whole mousse} - \frac{\boxed{}}{\boxed{}} = \frac{\boxed{}}{\boxed{}}$$

1
whole
mousse

Subtracting fractions

There are three bagels left in the bag.
Bruce wants to have one for breakfast today.
Complete the calculation to show the fraction
of the bag that will be left.

$$\frac{3}{5} - \frac{}{} = \frac{}{}$$

How many...?

This team is hard at work. Fill in the boxes to show the fraction of the group doing each activity.

Those little mice are very strong!

carrying a brick

painting

pushing a wheelbarrow

How many fish?

Fill in the boxes to show the fraction of the fish that are spotted.

spotted

Painted shapes

Draw a line to connect each painted
shape to the correct fraction.

$$\frac{5}{6}$$ painted $$\frac{2}{6}$$ painted $$\frac{1}{6}$$ painted $$\frac{3}{6}$$ painted

Dividing into sixths

Zeb has divided his seed tray into sixths.
Write the correct fraction inside each part.

Equal parts

The mice have divided their blocks of cheese into six pieces. Circle the cheese that is divided into sixths.

I don't think mine's right!

What fraction?

Look at the flower below. Then, fill in the boxes to show the fraction of the flower that has nibbles in it, and the fraction that does not.

with nibbles   no nibbles

Adding fractions

Bruce has placed four sixths of his lime tart
onto this plate. He has two more pieces to add.
Complete the calculation to show the fraction
of the tart that will be on the plate.

Wait a minute, Pat!

$$\frac{\quad}{\quad} + \frac{\quad}{\quad} = \frac{\quad}{\quad} \text{ or } 1$$

whole
tart

Adding fractions

Two sixths of these meerkats are wearing crowns. Draw a crown on another three of them. Now complete the calculation to show the fraction of the group wearing crowns.

Subtracting fractions

These friends have eaten three sixths of their apple cake. Complete the calculation to show the fraction of the cake that is left.

$$1 - \frac{\square}{\square} = \frac{\square}{\square}$$

whole cake

Subtracting fractions

The mice have found three sixths of a block of cheese. They will eat one of the sixths. Complete the calculation to show the fraction of the cheese that will be left.

$$\frac{3}{6} - \frac{}{} = \frac{}{}$$

How many...?

Fill in the boxes to show the fraction
of the group doing each activity.

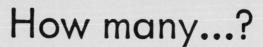

Catch,
Wolfy!

fishing

playing catch

eating
ice cream

How many teapots?

Fill in the boxes to show the fraction
of the teapots that have stars on them.

have stars

Painted shapes

Draw a line to connect each painted shape to the correct fraction.

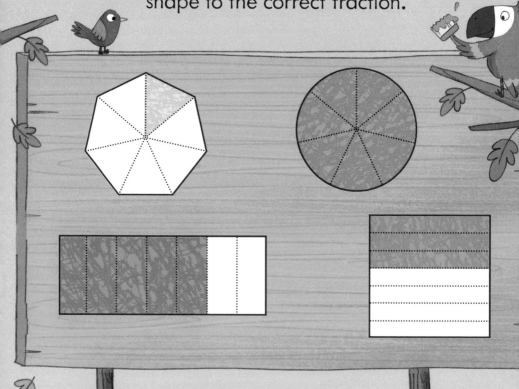

$$\frac{5}{7}$$ painted

$$\frac{1}{7}$$ painted

$$\frac{7}{7}$$ painted

$$\frac{3}{7}$$ painted

Dividing into sevenths

Zeb has divided his flowerbed into sevenths.
Write the correct fraction inside each part.

Equal parts

The animals have divided their fabrics into seven pieces. Circle the fabric that is divided into sevenths.

What fraction?

Look at the flower below. Then, fill in the boxes to show the fraction of the flower that has nibbles in it, and the fraction that does not.

with nibbles   no nibbles

Adding fractions

One seventh of these koalas are wearing top hats. Draw a top hat on another four of them, then complete the calculation to show the fraction of the group wearing top hats.

Adding fractions

There are seven slices of bread in a packet. Ping has two sevenths of the packet. Wolfy has four sevenths of the packet. Fill in the blank boxes to show the fraction of the packet they have altogether.

Subtracting fractions

There are four cookies left out of a box of seven. Hop is going to eat two of them. Complete the calculation to show the fraction of the box that will be left.

I love cookies!

Cookies

$$\frac{4}{7} - \frac{}{} = \frac{}{}$$

Subtracting fractions

These zebras were ready for their dance show,
but now five of them have lost their tutus!
Complete the calculation to show the
fraction of the group wearing tutus.

$$1 - \frac{}{} = \frac{}{}$$

whole
group

How many...?

Fill in the boxes to show the fraction
of the group doing each activity.

holding
balloons

dancing

eating cake

How many butterflies?

Fill in the boxes to show the fraction
of the butterflies that are blue.

blue

Painted shapes

Draw a line to connect each painted
shape to the correct fraction.

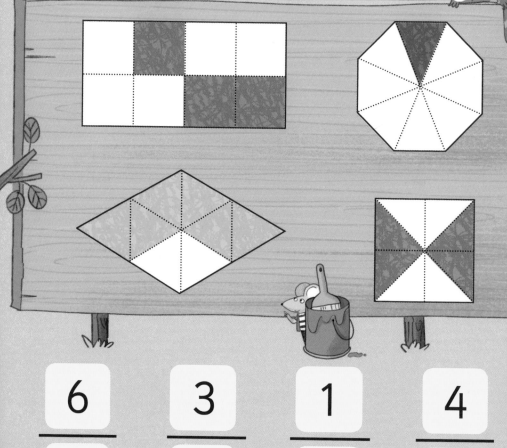

$$\frac{6}{8}$$ painted

$$\frac{3}{8}$$ painted

$$\frac{1}{8}$$ painted

$$\frac{4}{8}$$ painted

Dividing into eighths

Zeb has divided his flowerbed into eighths.
Write the correct fraction inside each part.

Equal parts

The animals have divided their brownies into eight pieces. Circle the brownie that is divided into eighths.

What fraction?

Look at the flower below. Then, fill in the boxes to show the fraction of the flower that has nibbles in it, and the fraction that does not.

with nibbles

no nibbles

Adding fractions

Pin has eaten four eighths of an orange and Hop has eaten three eighths. Complete the calculation to show the fraction of the orange they have eaten altogether.

Where's the last piece gone?

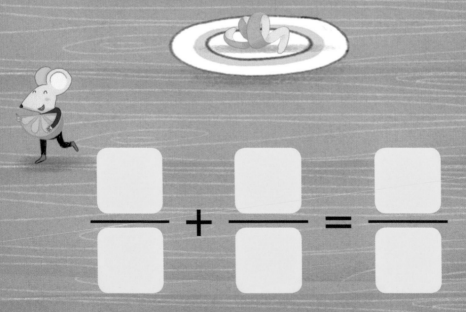

Adding fractions

Ping and Wolfy divided their melon into eight
equal pieces. They each have four pieces.
Complete the calculation to show the
fraction of the melon they have altogether.

$$\frac{}{} + \frac{}{} = \frac{}{} \quad \text{or} \quad 1$$

whole
melon

Kat has eaten two eighths of her apple. Complete the calculation to show the fraction of the apple that is left.

The mice have found five eighths of a leftover
fruit cake. They are going to eat three pieces of it.
Complete the calculation to show the fraction
of the cake that will be left.

$$\frac{5}{8} - \frac{}{} = \frac{}{}$$

How many...?

Fill in the boxes to show the fraction
of the group doing each activity.

taking
a bath

combing
their hair

brushing
their teeth

How many bugs?

Fill in the boxes to show the fraction
of the bugs that have spots.

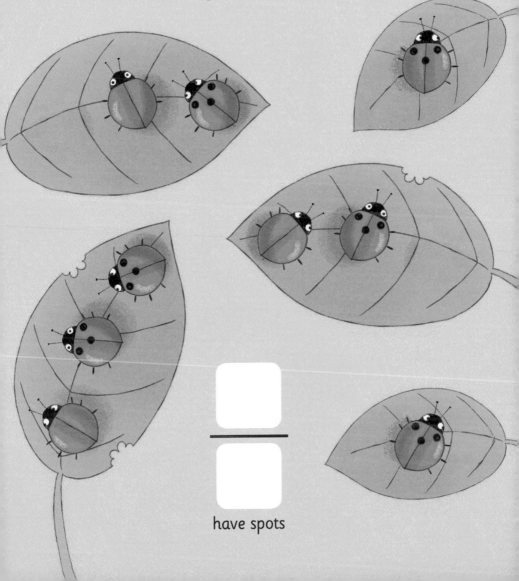

have spots

Draw a line to connect each painted
shape to the correct fraction.

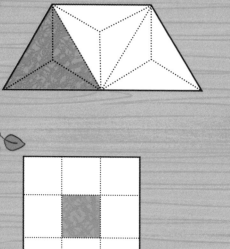

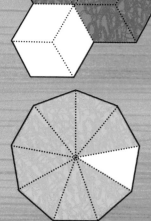

$$\frac{8}{9}$$ painted

$$\frac{3}{9}$$ painted

$$\frac{1}{9}$$ painted

$$\frac{6}{9}$$ painted

Dividing into ninths

Zeb has divided his flowerbed into ninths.
Write the correct fraction inside each part.

Careful with those seeds!

Equal parts

The mice have divided their flatbreads into nine portions. Circle the flatbread that is divided into ninths.

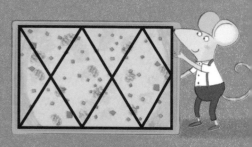

I love flatbread!

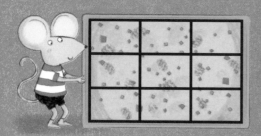

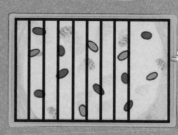

What fraction?

Look at the flower below. Then, fill in the boxes to show the fraction of the flower that has nibbles in it, and the fraction that does not.

with nibbles   no nibbles

Adding fractions

Five out of these nine mice are wearing striped T-shirts. Draw stripes on one more T-shirt. Complete the calculation to show the fraction of mice wearing striped T-shirts.

Adding fractions

Gloria has made a patchwork blanket for the mice.
Three patches are spotted. Draw spots on another
two patches, then complete the calculation to show
the fraction of the blanket that will be spotted.

Wolfy and Ping have bought a loaf of bread
and they are each having two slices of toast.
Complete the calculation to show the
fraction of the loaf that is left.

$$1 - \frac{4}{9} = \frac{}{}$$

Subtracting fractions

The mice have found six cookies left from a box of nine. They are going to eat four of them. Complete the calculation to show the fraction of the box that will be left.

$$\frac{6}{9} - \frac{}{} = \frac{}{}$$

How many...?

This group of friends is at the fair.
Fill in the boxes to show the fraction of
the group doing each activity.

tossing
rings

doing
archery

How many ducks?

Fill in the boxes to show the fraction of little ducks that are facing to the left.

facing left

Painted shapes

Draw a line to connect each painted
shape to the correct fraction.

$$\frac{2}{10}$$ painted

$$\frac{8}{10}$$ painted

$$\frac{4}{10}$$ painted

$$\frac{7}{10}$$ painted

Dividing into tenths

Zeb has divided his vegetable patch into tenths.
Write the correct fraction inside each part.

Equal parts

82

The animals have divided their sponge cakes into ten portions. Circle the cake that is divided into tenths.

What fraction?

Look at the flower below. Then, fill in the boxes to show the fraction of the flower that has nibbles in it, and the fraction that does not.

with nibbles   no nibbles

Adding fractions

Zeb has painted two tenths of this fence red and Hop has painted four tenths blue. Complete the calculation to show the fraction of the fence that is painted.

$$\frac{}{} + \frac{}{} = \frac{}{}$$

Adding fractions

Ping is laying a path with ten slabs. He has laid eight tenths of the path and has two slabs still to lay. Complete the calculation to show the fraction of the path that will be built once they are laid.

$$\frac{}{} + \frac{}{} = \frac{}{}$$ or **1**

whole path

Together, Pin, Hop and Pat have three tenths of Bruce's homemade orange tart. Complete the calculation to show the fraction of the tart that is left.

$$1 - \frac{3}{10} = \frac{}{}$$

whole
tart

Subtracting fractions

Zeb and Pin are sharing a pizza. They have eaten six tenths of it so far. Complete the calculation to show the fraction of the pizza that is left.

whole
pizza

Equivalent fractions

Look at the shaded parts of each circle, then draw
lines to match up pairs of equivalent fractions.

$$\frac{3}{9}$$

$$\frac{2}{10}$$

$$\frac{1}{2}$$

$$\frac{3}{6}$$

$$\frac{2}{6}$$

$$\frac{1}{5}$$

Unit fractions

A unit fraction is one part of a whole.
Circle all the unit fractions below.

$$\frac{6}{9}$$

$$\frac{1}{5}$$

$$\frac{1}{3}$$

$$\frac{3}{4}$$

$$\frac{1}{8}$$

Hello!

$$\frac{4}{4}$$

Fractions match-up

Draw a line from each fraction
to its matching cloud.

$\dfrac{3}{4}$

seven ninths

$\dfrac{5}{7}$

$\dfrac{6}{10}$

one half

six tenths

three quarters

$\dfrac{1}{2}$

$\dfrac{7}{9}$

five sevenths

Draw a line to connect all these plates in order.
Start with the plate that has the smallest fraction
of cake and finish with the largest.

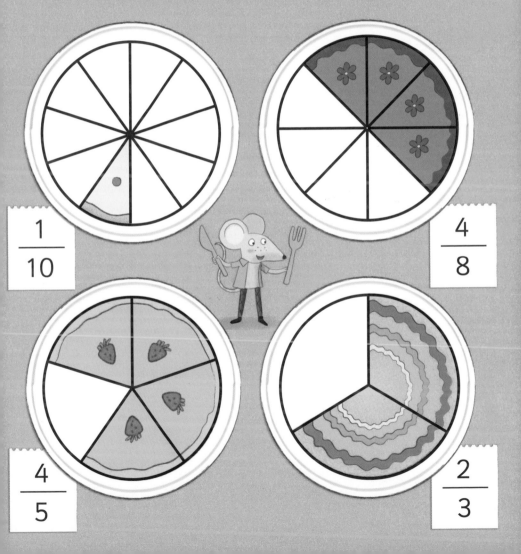

$\dfrac{1}{10}$

$\dfrac{4}{8}$

$\dfrac{4}{5}$

$\dfrac{2}{3}$

Equivalent fractions

Look at the shaded parts of each circle, then draw
lines to match up pairs of equivalent fractions.

$\dfrac{4}{6}$

$\dfrac{4}{8}$

$\dfrac{2}{4}$

$\dfrac{1}{4}$

$\dfrac{2}{8}$

$\dfrac{2}{3}$

Unit fractions

A unit fraction is one part of a whole.
Circle all the unit fractions below.

$$\frac{7}{10}$$

$$\frac{1}{8}$$

$$\frac{3}{5}$$

$$\frac{4}{4}$$

$$\frac{5}{7}$$

$$\frac{1}{5}$$

Fractions match-up

Draw a line from each fraction
to its matching cloud.

four ninths

$\dfrac{3}{6}$

$\dfrac{2}{8}$

eight tenths

three sixths

four sevenths

$\dfrac{4}{9}$

$\dfrac{4}{7}$

$\dfrac{8}{10}$

two eighths

Ordering fractions

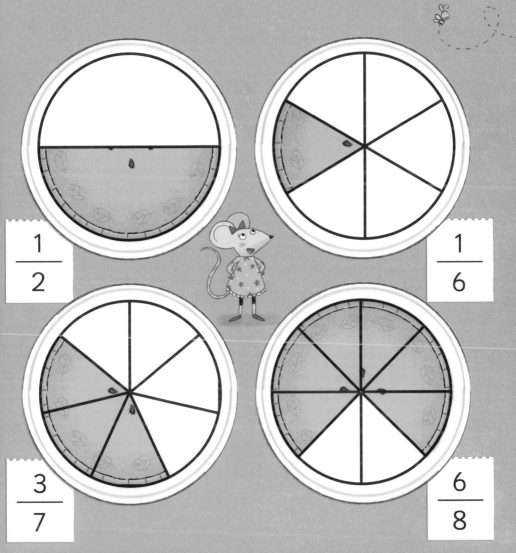

Draw a line to connect all these plates in order.
Start with the plate that has the smallest fraction
of pie and finish with the largest.

$\frac{1}{2}$

$\frac{1}{6}$

$\frac{3}{7}$

$\frac{6}{8}$

Equivalent fractions

Look at the shaded parts of each circle, then draw lines to match up pairs of equivalent fractions.

$$\frac{6}{9}$$

$$\frac{3}{6}$$

$$\frac{4}{6}$$

$$\frac{5}{10}$$

$$\frac{8}{10}$$

$$\frac{4}{5}$$

Equivalent fractions

Help the mice match up these balloons. Draw
lines to pair them into equivalent fractions.

Ordering fractions

Draw a line to connect all these plates in order. Start with the plate that has the smallest fraction of cheese and finish with the largest.

$\dfrac{3}{9}$

$\dfrac{1}{5}$

$\dfrac{2}{7}$

$\dfrac{4}{6}$

Equivalent fractions

Look at the shaded parts of each circle, then draw
lines to match up pairs of equivalent fractions.

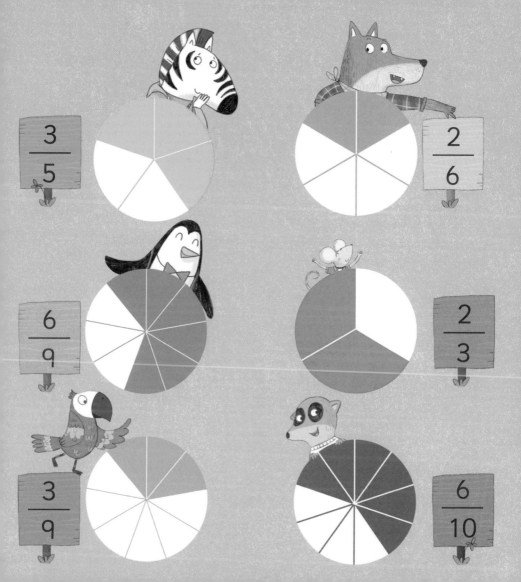

$\dfrac{3}{5}$

$\dfrac{2}{6}$

$\dfrac{6}{9}$

$\dfrac{2}{3}$

$\dfrac{3}{9}$

$\dfrac{6}{10}$

Equivalent fractions

Help the mice match up these kites. Draw lines
to pair them into equivalent fractions.

Ordering fractions

Draw a line to connect all these plates in order. Start with the plate that has the smallest fraction of mousse and finish with the largest.

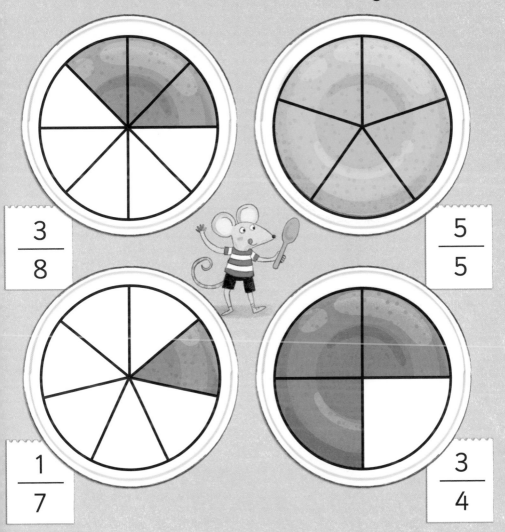

$\dfrac{3}{8}$

$\dfrac{5}{5}$

$\dfrac{1}{7}$

$\dfrac{3}{4}$

Equivalent fractions

Look at the shaded parts of each circle, then draw
lines to match up pairs of equivalent fractions.

Equivalent fractions

Help the mice match up these kites. Draw lines
to pair them into equivalent fractions.

Ordering fractions

Draw a line to connect all these plates in order.
Start with the plate that has the smallest fraction
of pizza and finish with the largest.

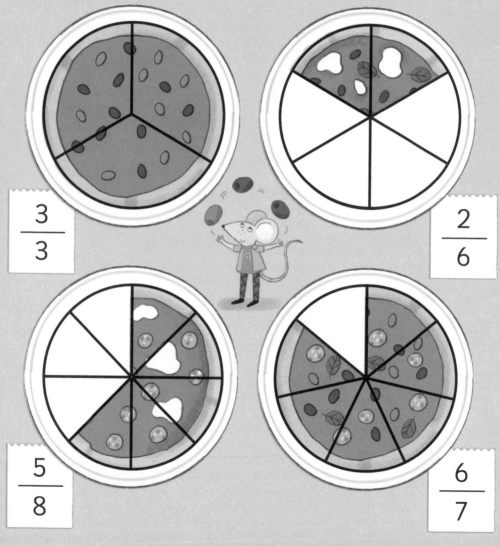

$\dfrac{3}{3}$

$\dfrac{2}{6}$

$\dfrac{5}{8}$

$\dfrac{6}{7}$

Equivalent fractions

Help the mice match up these balloons. Draw lines to pair them into equivalent fractions.

Ordering fractions

Draw a line to connect these fractions in order of size, starting with the smallest and finishing with the largest.

$\dfrac{3}{4}$

$\dfrac{7}{9}$

$\dfrac{4}{8}$

$\dfrac{2}{5}$

Equivalent fractions

Help the mice match up these signs. Draw lines
to pair them into equivalent fractions.

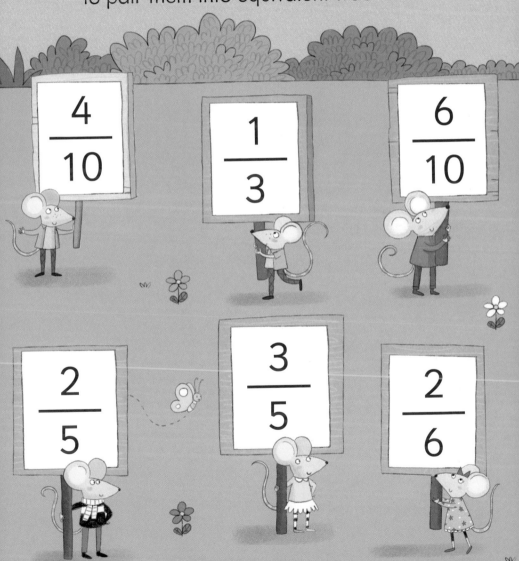

Ordering fractions

Draw a line to connect these fractions in order of size, starting with the smallest and finishing with the largest.

$$\frac{1}{2}$$

$$\frac{2}{8}$$

$$\frac{5}{6}$$

$$\frac{10}{10}$$

True or false?

Read the statements below, and write a 'T' next to the ones that are true, and an 'F' next to the ones that are false.

$\dfrac{3}{6}$ is equivalent to $\dfrac{1}{2}$

$\dfrac{4}{8}$ is equivalent to $\dfrac{3}{5}$

$\dfrac{1}{3}$ is equivalent to $\dfrac{2}{6}$

$\dfrac{7}{7}$ is equivalent to $\dfrac{9}{10}$

Ordering fractions

Draw a line to connect these fractions in order of size, starting with the smallest and finishing with the largest.

$$\frac{3}{5}$$

$$\frac{1}{9}$$

$$\frac{4}{4}$$

$$\frac{7}{8}$$

True or false?

Read the statements below, and write a 'T' next to the ones that are true, and an 'F' next to the ones that are false.

$\dfrac{2}{3}$ is equivalent to $\dfrac{5}{8}$

$\dfrac{5}{10}$ is equivalent to $\dfrac{2}{4}$

$\dfrac{1}{4}$ is equivalent to $\dfrac{2}{8}$

$\dfrac{3}{5}$ is equivalent to $\dfrac{4}{6}$

Ordering fractions

Draw a line to connect these fractions in order of size, starting with the smallest and finishing with the largest.

$$\frac{9}{10}$$

$$\frac{4}{9}$$

$$\frac{1}{4}$$

$$\frac{4}{5}$$

True or false?

Read the statements below, and write a 'T' next to the ones that are true, and an 'F' next to the ones that are false.

$\dfrac{2}{10}$ is equivalent to $\dfrac{1}{5}$

$\dfrac{2}{3}$ is equivalent to $\dfrac{6}{9}$

$\dfrac{4}{6}$ is equivalent to $\dfrac{2}{4}$

$\dfrac{1}{4}$ is equivalent to $\dfrac{4}{8}$

Ordering fractions

Draw a line to connect these fractions in order of size, starting with the smallest and finishing with the largest.

True or false?

Read the statements below, and write a 'T' next to the ones that are true, and an 'F' next to the ones that are false.

$\dfrac{1}{3}$ is equivalent to $\dfrac{2}{9}$

$\dfrac{6}{8}$ is equivalent to $\dfrac{3}{4}$

$\dfrac{6}{9}$ is equivalent to $\dfrac{3}{3}$

$\dfrac{4}{5}$ is equivalent to $\dfrac{8}{10}$

Word problems

Answer these word problems by writing the
correct fractions in the blank boxes.

One half of the children in the class have a
packed lunch, and the rest have a school lunch.
Write the fraction that have a school lunch.

———

One quarter of the animals on the bus are
listening to music, and the rest are chatting.
Write the fraction that are chatting.

———

Three quarters of the eggs in the carton are
brown, and the rest are white. Write the
fraction that are white.

———

One half of the ducks on the pond are male,
and the rest are female. Write the fraction
that are female.

———

Halves

Write the answers to these questions in the boxes.

$\frac{1}{2}$ of 10 = ☐　　$\frac{1}{2}$ of 90 = ☐

$\frac{1}{2}$ of 30 = ☐　　$\frac{1}{2}$ of 26 = ☐

$\frac{1}{2}$ of 48 = ☐　　$\frac{1}{2}$ of 64 = ☐

What is half of
each of these
numbers?

$\frac{1}{2}$ of 18 = ☐

We'll need to
divide each
number by two.

Word problems

Answer these word problems by writing the correct fractions in the blank boxes.

One third of the roses in Kat's vase are red, and the rest are white. Write the fraction that are white.

Two fifths of the pirates on the ship have beards, and the rest do not. Write the fraction that do not have beards.

Four fifths of the candles on Wolfy's birthday cake are lit, and the rest are not. Write the fraction that are not lit.

Two thirds of the sheep in the field are lying down, and the rest are standing. Write the fraction that are standing.

Write the answers to these questions in the boxes.

$\frac{1}{4}$ of 20 =

$\frac{2}{4}$ of 36 =

$\frac{2}{4}$ of 14 =

$\frac{1}{4}$ of 16 =

$\frac{3}{4}$ of 44 =

$\frac{3}{4}$ of 8 =

First, divide each number by four...

$\frac{1}{4}$ of 28 =

...then you'll know what one quarter of the number is.

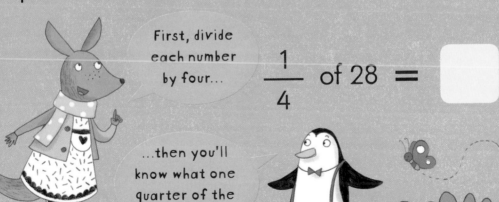

Word problems

Answer these word problems by writing the correct fractions in the blank boxes.

Four tenths of the pins in the bowling lane are standing, and Zeb has knocked the rest down. Write the fraction that have been knocked down.

Three eighths of the nuts in Pat's jar are hazelnuts, and the rest are almonds. Write the fraction that are almonds.

Eight tenths of the butterflies in the garden are orange, and the rest are purple. Write the fraction of the butterflies that are purple.

Two sixths of the animals in the pool are wearing goggles, and the rest are not. Write the fraction that are not wearing goggles.

Thirds

Write the answers to these questions in the boxes.

$\frac{1}{3}$ of 9 = ☐ $\frac{1}{3}$ of 30 = ☐

$\frac{1}{3}$ of 27 = ☐ $\frac{2}{3}$ of 60 = ☐

$\frac{2}{3}$ of 21 = ☐ $\frac{2}{3}$ of 12 = ☐

First, divide each number by three...

$\frac{1}{3}$ of 18 = ☐

...then you'll know what one third of the number is.

Word problems

Answer these word problems by writing the
correct fractions in the blank boxes.

Five sevenths of the boats on the lake
have sails, and the rest have oars. Write
the fraction that have oars.

Six ninths of the rabbits in the warren
are sleeping. Write the fraction that
are awake.

Six sevenths of the trees in the park are
oak trees, and the rest are beech trees.
Write the fraction that are beech trees.

Three ninths of the seats on the train are
occupied, and the rest are empty. Write
the fraction that are empty.

Fifths

Write the answers to these questions in the boxes.

$\frac{1}{5}$ of 5 = [ ] $\frac{3}{5}$ of 40 = [ ]

$\frac{2}{5}$ of 15 = [ ] $\frac{2}{5}$ of 20 = [ ]

$\frac{4}{5}$ of 35 = [ ] $\frac{3}{5}$ of 25 = [ ]

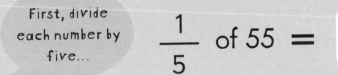

First, divide each number by five...

$\frac{1}{5}$ of 55 = [ ]

...then you'll know what one fifth of the number is.

Word problems

Answer these word problems by writing the correct numbers in the blank boxes.

There are twenty birds in the tree. Half are singing and the rest are building nests. How many are building nests?

There are thirty-five vehicles on the road. Two fifths are trucks, and the rest are cars. How many are cars?

There are fourteen cookies in Ping's tin. Four sevenths are milk chocolate, and the rest are dark chocolate. How many are dark chocolate?

There are sixty marbles in Bruce's bag. Five tenths are green, and the rest are blue. How many of the marbles are blue?

Sixths

Write the answers to these questions in the boxes.

$\dfrac{1}{6}$ of 36 =

$\dfrac{4}{6}$ of 6 =

$\dfrac{3}{6}$ of 18 =

$\dfrac{5}{6}$ of 12 =

$\dfrac{2}{6}$ of 24 =

$\dfrac{1}{6}$ of 42 =

$\dfrac{3}{6}$ of 30 =

First, divide each number by six...

...then you'll know what one sixth of the number is.

Word problems

Answer these word problems by writing the correct numbers in the blank boxes.

There are eighteen jars on the shelf. Two thirds contain strawberry jam, and the rest contain raspberry. How many contain raspberry jam?

There are forty-eight trains in Hop's toy box. Four sixths are red, and the rest are green. How many of the trains are green?

There are twenty-seven hikers on the mountain. Six ninths are walking up the mountain, and the rest are walking down. How many are walking down?

There are fourteen glasses on the table. Half are filled with juice, and the rest are empty. How many glasses are empty?

Eighths

Write the answers to these questions in the boxes.

$\frac{1}{8}$ of 48 = ☐

$\frac{2}{8}$ of 16 = ☐

$\frac{5}{8}$ of 40 = ☐

$\frac{3}{8}$ of 32 = ☐

$\frac{7}{8}$ of 80 = ☐

$\frac{4}{8}$ of 8 = ☐

$\frac{6}{8}$ of 24 = ☐

First, divide each number by eight...

...then you'll know what one eighth of the number is.

Word problems

Answer these word problems by writing the correct numbers in the blank boxes.

There are twenty-four hot-air balloons in the sky. Three quarters are orange, and the rest are purple. How many are purple?

There are forty-two people at the beach. Six sevenths are sunbathing, and the rest are swimming in the sea. How many are swimming?

There are fifty singers in the school choir. Four tenths of them are boys, and the rest are girls. How many are girls?

There are sixty-six people at the match. Two thirds support the red team, and the rest support the blue team. How many support the blue team?

Tenths

Write the answers to these questions in the boxes.

$\frac{1}{10}$ of 30 =

$\frac{8}{10}$ of 70 =

$\frac{4}{10}$ of 80 =

$\frac{3}{10}$ of 40 =

$\frac{2}{10}$ of 40 =

$\frac{6}{10}$ of 60 =

First, divide each number by ten...

...then you'll know what one tenth of the number is.

$\frac{7}{10}$ of 20 =

$\frac{5}{10}$ of 50 =

Hop has one glass of juice and Pin has half a glass of juice. Together they have one and a half glasses of juice. Trace over the numbers to show how much juice they have.

1 glass of juice

$\frac{1}{2}$ a glass of juice

$= 1\frac{1}{2}$ glasses of juice

Pat has one glass of juice and Bruce has half a glass of juice. How much juice do they have altogether?

= ☐ —— glasses of juice

Quarters beyond 1

Hop has one glass of juice, and Pin has one quarter of a glass of juice. How much juice do they have altogether?

I'm really thirsty Hop!

= ⬜ □/□ glasses of juice

Pat has one glass of juice and Bruce has three quarters of a glass of juice. How much juice do they have altogether?

glasses of juice

Thirds beyond 1

Pin has one glass of juice, and Hop has two thirds of a glass of juice. How much juice do they have altogether?

= ⬜ $\dfrac{⬜}{⬜}$ glasses of juice

Pin has one glass of juice and Hop has one third of a glass of juice. How much juice do they have altogether?

= [ ] $\frac{[\ ]}{[\ ]}$ glasses of juice

Fraction wall

This wall shows how each fraction fits into one whole.
You can use it to help you with the activities in this pad.

| Whole | 1 | | | | | | | | | |

| Halves | $\dfrac{1}{2}$ | $\dfrac{1}{2}$ |

| Thirds | $\dfrac{1}{3}$ | $\dfrac{1}{3}$ | $\dfrac{1}{3}$ |

| Quarters | $\dfrac{1}{4}$ | $\dfrac{1}{4}$ | $\dfrac{1}{4}$ | $\dfrac{1}{4}$ |

| Fifths | $\dfrac{1}{5}$ | $\dfrac{1}{5}$ | $\dfrac{1}{5}$ | $\dfrac{1}{5}$ | $\dfrac{1}{5}$ |

| Sixths | $\dfrac{1}{6}$ | $\dfrac{1}{6}$ | $\dfrac{1}{6}$ | $\dfrac{1}{6}$ | $\dfrac{1}{6}$ | $\dfrac{1}{6}$ |

| Sevenths | $\dfrac{1}{7}$ | $\dfrac{1}{7}$ | $\dfrac{1}{7}$ | $\dfrac{1}{7}$ | $\dfrac{1}{7}$ | $\dfrac{1}{7}$ | $\dfrac{1}{7}$ |

| Eighths | $\dfrac{1}{8}$ | $\dfrac{1}{8}$ | $\dfrac{1}{8}$ | $\dfrac{1}{8}$ | $\dfrac{1}{8}$ | $\dfrac{1}{8}$ | $\dfrac{1}{8}$ | $\dfrac{1}{8}$ |

| Ninths | $\dfrac{1}{9}$ | $\dfrac{1}{9}$ | $\dfrac{1}{9}$ | $\dfrac{1}{9}$ | $\dfrac{1}{9}$ | $\dfrac{1}{9}$ | $\dfrac{1}{9}$ | $\dfrac{1}{9}$ | $\dfrac{1}{9}$ |

| Tenths | $\dfrac{1}{10}$ | $\dfrac{1}{10}$ | $\dfrac{1}{10}$ | $\dfrac{1}{10}$ | $\dfrac{1}{10}$ | $\dfrac{1}{10}$ | $\dfrac{1}{10}$ | $\dfrac{1}{10}$ | $\dfrac{1}{10}$ | $\dfrac{1}{10}$ |

Answers

How many...? 1
Fill in the boxes to show what these four friends are doing.

2 out of 4 are singing

2 out of 4 are sitting

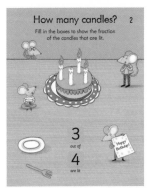

How many candles? 2
Fill in the boxes to show the fraction of the candles that are lit.

3 out of 4 are lit

Happy Birthday!

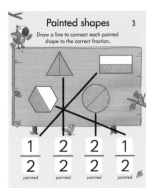

Painted shapes 3
Draw a line to connect each painted shape to the correct fraction.

$\frac{1}{2}$ painted $\frac{2}{2}$ painted $\frac{2}{2}$ painted $\frac{1}{2}$ painted

Painted shapes 4
Draw a line to connect each painted shape to the correct fraction.

$\frac{2}{4}$ painted $\frac{1}{4}$ painted $\frac{4}{4}$ painted $\frac{3}{4}$ painted

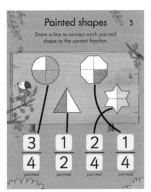

Painted shapes 5
Draw a line to connect each painted shape to the correct fraction.

$\frac{3}{4}$ painted $\frac{1}{2}$ painted $\frac{2}{4}$ painted $\frac{1}{4}$ painted

Dividing into halves 6
Zeb has divided his vegetable patch into halves. Write the correct fraction inside each part.

$\frac{1}{2}$ $\frac{1}{2}$

Dividing into quarters 7
Zeb has divided his flowerbed into quarters. Write the correct fraction inside each part.

$\frac{1}{4}$ $\frac{1}{4}$

$\frac{1}{4}$ $\frac{1}{4}$

Equal parts 8
The animals have divided their cakes into two pieces. Circle the cake that is divided into halves.

Equal parts 9
The animals have divided their cakes into four pieces. Circle the cake that is divided into quarters.

Answers

What fraction? 10

Look at the flower below. Then, fill in the boxes to show the fraction of the flower that has nibbles in it, and the fraction that does not.

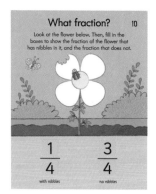

$$\frac{1}{4} \qquad \frac{3}{4}$$

with nibbles   no nibbles

Adding fractions 11

Wolfy and Ping each have half a pizza. They want to put their halves together on one plate. Complete the calculation to show how much pizza they will have altogether.

$$\frac{1}{2} + \frac{1}{2} = \frac{2}{2} \text{ or } 1$$

whole pizza

Adding fractions 12

Bruce and Hop love the apple pie at the café. They each have one quarter of it. Complete the calculation to show the fraction of the pie they have altogether.

$$\frac{1}{4} + \frac{1}{4} = \frac{2}{4}$$

Adding fractions 13

Gloria has decorated three quarters of her cake. Decorate the other quarter for her, then complete the calculation to show the fraction of her cake that is decorated.

$$\frac{3}{4} + \frac{1}{4} = \frac{4}{4} \text{ or } 1$$

whole cake

Subtracting fractions 14

Kat cut her tomato into quarters. She has eaten three quarters. Complete the calculation to show the fraction of the tomato she has left.

$$1 \text{ or } \frac{4}{4} - \frac{3}{4} = \frac{1}{4}$$

whole tomato

Subtracting fractions 15

Zeb and Ping are sharing an egg sandwich. Zeb has eaten two quarters of it. Complete the calculation to show the fraction of the sandwich left for Ping.

$$1 \text{ or } \frac{4}{4} - \frac{2}{4} = \frac{2}{4}$$

whole sandwich

Subtracting fractions 16

Zeb, Pat and Kat have eaten half a lemon cake between them. Complete the calculation to show the fraction of cake that is left.

$$1 - \frac{1}{2} = \frac{1}{2}$$

whole cake

What fraction? 17

Gloria has fruit for lunch. Fill in the blank boxes to show the fraction of her lunchbox that contains each fruit.

$$\frac{1}{4} \qquad \frac{2}{4} \qquad \frac{1}{4}$$

banana   grapes   strawberries

How many...? 18

Fill in the boxes to show the fraction of the group doing each activity.

$$\frac{1}{3} \qquad \frac{2}{3}$$

watering plants   digging

Answers

How many flowers? 19

Pat has three flowers. Fill in the boxes to show the fraction of his flowers that are red.

$\frac{2}{3}$ red

Painted shapes 20

Draw a line to connect each painted shape to the correct fraction.

$\frac{2}{3}$ painted $\frac{1}{3}$ painted $\frac{3}{3}$ painted $\frac{2}{3}$ painted

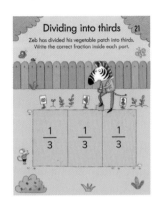

Dividing into thirds 21

Zeb has divided his vegetable patch into thirds. Write the correct fraction inside each part.

$\frac{1}{3}$ $\frac{1}{3}$ $\frac{1}{3}$

Equal parts 22

The animals have divided their cakes into three pieces. Circle the cake that is divided into thirds.

What fraction? 23

Look at the flower below. Then, fill in the boxes to show the fraction of the flower that has nibbles in it, and the fraction that does not.

$\frac{2}{3}$ with nibbles $\frac{1}{3}$ no nibbles

Adding fractions 24

One third of these penguins are wearing bow ties. Draw a bow tie on another penguin, then complete the calculation to show the fraction of the group wearing bow ties.

$\frac{1}{3} + \frac{1}{3} = \frac{2}{3}$

Adding fractions 25

Zeb has placed two thirds of his lemon cake onto a plate and has another third to add. Complete the calculation to show the fraction of cake that will be on the plate.

$\frac{2}{3} + \frac{1}{3} = \frac{3}{3}$ or 1 whole cake

Subtracting fractions 26

Wolfy is hungry today. He has eaten two thirds of the café's fish pie. Complete the calculation to show the fraction of pie that is left.

$1 - \frac{2}{3} = \frac{1}{3}$ whole pie

Subtracting fractions 27

The mice have found two thirds of a fruit loaf. They will eat one of the thirds. Complete the calculation to show the fraction of fruit loaf that will be left.

$\frac{2}{3} - \frac{1}{3} = \frac{1}{3}$

Answers

How many...? 28

These friends are working on articles and pictures for their magazine. Fill in the boxes to show the fraction of the group doing each activity.

$$\frac{2}{5}$$ painting

$$\frac{3}{5}$$ writing

How many flags? 29

Fill in the boxes to show the fraction of the flags that have stripes.

$$\frac{3}{5}$$ with stripes

Painted shapes 30

Draw a line to connect each painted shape to the correct fraction.

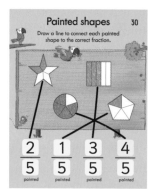

$$\frac{2}{5}$$ painted

$$\frac{1}{5}$$ painted

$$\frac{3}{5}$$ painted

$$\frac{4}{5}$$ painted

Dividing into fifths 31

Zeb has divided his flowerbed into fifths. Write the correct fraction inside each part.

$$\frac{1}{5} \quad \frac{1}{5} \quad \frac{1}{5} \quad \frac{1}{5} \quad \frac{1}{5}$$

Equal parts 32

The mice have divided their blocks of cheese into five pieces. Circle the block of cheese that is divided into fifths.

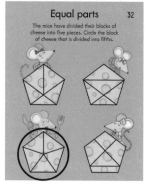

What fraction? 33

Look at the flower below. Then, fill in the boxes to show the fraction of the flower that has nibbles in it, and the fraction that does not.

$$\frac{4}{5}$$ with nibbles

$$\frac{1}{5}$$ no nibbles

Adding fractions 34

Bruce has decorated two fifths of his brownie with dark chocolate and will decorate the rest with white chocolate. Complete the calculation to show the fraction of brownie that will be decorated with chocolate.

$$\frac{2}{5} + \frac{3}{5} = \frac{5}{5}$$ or 1 whole brownie

Adding fractions 35

Pin has one fifth of Zeb's birthday cake. Zeb has eaten too much and gives Pin his fifth, too. Complete the calculation to show the fraction of the cake Pin has altogether.

$$\frac{1}{5} + \frac{1}{5} = \frac{2}{5}$$

Subtracting fractions 36

Hop has eaten two fifths of her mousse. Complete the calculation to show the fraction of mousse she has left.

$$1 - \frac{2}{5} = \frac{3}{5}$$ whole mousse

Answers

Subtracting fractions 37

There are three bagels left in the bag. Bruce wants to have one for breakfast today. Complete the calculation to show the fraction of the bag that will be left.

$$\frac{3}{5} - \frac{1}{5} = \frac{2}{5}$$

How many...? 38

This team is hard at work. Fill in the boxes to show the fraction of the group doing each activity.

$$\frac{2}{6}$$ carrying a brick

$$\frac{3}{6}$$ painting

$$\frac{1}{6}$$ pushing a wheelbarrow

How many fish? 39

Fill in the boxes to show the fraction of the fish that are spotted.

$$\frac{3}{6}$$ spotted

Painted shapes 40

Draw a line to connect each painted shape to the correct fraction.

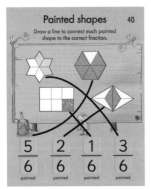

$$\frac{5}{6}$$ painted

$$\frac{2}{6}$$ painted

$$\frac{1}{6}$$ painted

$$\frac{3}{6}$$ painted

Dividing into sixths 41

Zeb has divided his seed tray into sixths. Write the correct fraction inside each part.

$$\frac{1}{6} \quad \frac{1}{6} \quad \frac{1}{6}$$
$$\frac{1}{6} \quad \frac{1}{6} \quad \frac{1}{6}$$

Equal parts 42

The mice have divided their blocks of cheese into six pieces. Circle the cheese that is divided into sixths.

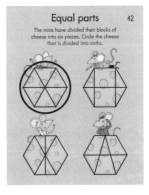

What fraction? 43

Look at the flower below. Then, fill in the boxes to show the fraction of the flower that has nibbles in it, and the fraction that does not.

$$\frac{1}{6}$$ with nibbles

$$\frac{5}{6}$$ no nibbles

Adding fractions 44

Bruce has placed four sixths of his lime tart onto this plate. He has two more pieces to add. Complete the calculation to show the fraction of the tart that will be on the plate.

$$\frac{4}{6} + \frac{2}{6} = \frac{6}{6}$$ or 1 whole tart

Adding fractions 45

Two sixths of these meerkats are wearing crowns. Draw a crown on another three of them. Now complete the calculation to show the fraction of the group wearing crowns.

$$\frac{2}{6} + \frac{3}{6} = \frac{5}{6}$$

Answers

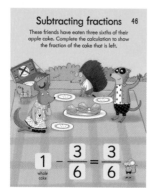

Subtracting fractions 46

These friends have eaten three sixths of their apple cake. Complete the calculation to show the fraction of the cake that is left.

$$1 - \frac{3}{6} = \frac{3}{6}$$

whole cake

Subtracting fractions 47

The mice have found three sixths of a block of cheese. They will eat one of the sixths. Complete the calculation to show the fraction of the cheese that will be left.

$$\frac{3}{6} - \frac{1}{6} = \frac{2}{6}$$

How many...? 48

Fill in the boxes to show the fraction of the group doing each activity.

$$\frac{4}{7} \qquad \frac{2}{7} \qquad \frac{1}{7}$$

fishing   playing catch   eating ice cream

How many teapots? 49

Fill in the boxes to show the fraction of the teapots that have stars on them.

$$\frac{2}{7}$$

have stars

Painted shapes 50

Draw a line to connect each painted shape to the correct fraction.

$$\frac{5}{7} \qquad \frac{1}{7} \qquad \frac{7}{7} \qquad \frac{3}{7}$$

painted   painted   painted   painted

Dividing into sevenths 51

Zeb has divided his flowerbed into sevenths. Write the correct fraction inside each part.

$$\frac{1}{7} \quad \frac{1}{7} \quad \frac{1}{7} \quad \frac{1}{7} \quad \frac{1}{7} \quad \frac{1}{7} \quad \frac{1}{7}$$

Equal parts 52

The animals have divided their fabrics into seven pieces. Circle the fabric that is divided into sevenths.

What fraction? 53

Look at the flower below. Then, fill in the boxes to show the fraction of the flower that has nibbles in it, and the fraction that does not.

$$\frac{3}{7} \qquad \frac{4}{7}$$

with nibbles   no nibbles

Adding fractions 54

One seventh of these koalas are wearing top hats. Draw a top hat on another four of them, then complete the calculation to show the fraction of the group wearing top hats.

$$\frac{1}{7} + \frac{4}{7} = \frac{5}{7}$$

Answers

Adding fractions 55

There are seven slices of bread in a packet. Ping has two sevenths of the packet. Wolfy has four sevenths of the packet. Fill in the blank boxes to show the fraction of the packet they have altogether.

$$\frac{2}{7} + \frac{4}{7} = \frac{6}{7}$$

Subtracting fractions 56

There are four cookies left out of a box of seven. Hop is going to eat two of them. Complete the calculation to show the fraction of the box that will be left.

$$\frac{4}{7} - \frac{2}{7} = \frac{2}{7}$$

Subtracting fractions 57

These zebras were ready for their dance show, but now five of them have lost their tutus! Complete the calculation to show the fraction of the group wearing tutus.

$$1 - \frac{5}{7} = \frac{2}{7}$$
whole group

How many...? 58

Fill in the boxes to show the fraction of the group doing each activity.

$$\frac{2}{8} \quad \frac{4}{8} \quad \frac{2}{8}$$
holding balloons   dancing   eating cake

How many butterflies? 59

Fill in the boxes to show the fraction of the butterflies that are blue.

$$\frac{4}{8}$$
blue

Painted shapes 60

Draw a line to connect each painted shape to the correct fraction.

$$\frac{6}{8} \quad \frac{3}{8} \quad \frac{1}{8} \quad \frac{4}{8}$$
painted   painted   painted   painted

Dividing into eighths 61

Zeb has divided his flowerbed into eighths. Write the correct fraction inside each part.

$$\frac{1}{8} \quad \frac{1}{8} \quad \frac{1}{8} \quad \frac{1}{8}$$
$$\frac{1}{8} \quad \frac{1}{8} \quad \frac{1}{8} \quad \frac{1}{8}$$

Equal parts 62

The animals have divided their brownies into eight pieces. Circle the brownie that is divided into eighths.

What fraction? 63

Look at the flower below. Then, fill in the boxes to show the fraction of the flower that has nibbles in it, and the fraction that does not.

$$\frac{5}{8} \quad \frac{3}{8}$$
with nibbles   no nibbles

Answers

Adding fractions 64

Pin has eaten four eighths of an orange and Hop has eaten three eighths. Complete the calculation to show the fraction of the orange they have eaten altogether.

$$\frac{4}{8} + \frac{3}{8} = \frac{7}{8}$$

Adding fractions 65

Ping and Wolfy divided their melon into eight equal pieces. They each have four pieces. Complete the calculation to show the fraction of the melon they have altogether.

$$\frac{4}{8} + \frac{4}{8} = \frac{8}{8} \text{ or } 1 \text{ whole melon}$$

Subtracting fractions 66

Kat has eaten two eighths of her apple. Complete the calculation to show the fraction of the apple that is left.

$$1 \text{ whole apple} - \frac{2}{8} = \frac{6}{8}$$

Subtracting fractions 67

The mice have found five eighths of a leftover fruit cake. They are going to eat three pieces of it. Complete the calculation to show the fraction of the cake that will be left.

$$\frac{5}{8} - \frac{3}{8} = \frac{2}{8}$$

How many...? 68

Fill in the boxes to show the fraction of the group doing each activity.

$$\frac{3}{9} \quad \frac{3}{9} \quad \frac{3}{9}$$

taking a bath   combing their hair   brushing their teeth

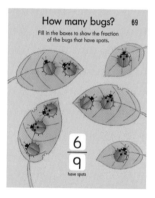

How many bugs? 69

Fill in the boxes to show the fraction of the bugs that have spots.

$$\frac{6}{9}$$

have spots

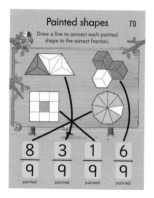

Painted shapes 70

Draw a line to connect each painted shape to the correct fraction.

$$\frac{8}{9} \quad \frac{3}{9} \quad \frac{1}{9} \quad \frac{6}{9}$$

painted   painted   painted   painted

Dividing into ninths 71

Zeb has divided his flowerbed into ninths. Write the correct fraction inside each part.

$\frac{1}{9}$	$\frac{1}{9}$	$\frac{1}{9}$
$\frac{1}{9}$	$\frac{1}{9}$	$\frac{1}{9}$
$\frac{1}{9}$	$\frac{1}{9}$	$\frac{1}{9}$

Equal parts 72

The mice have divided their flatbreads into nine portions. Circle the flatbread that is divided into ninths.

Answers

What fraction? 73

Look at the flower below. Then, fill in the boxes to show the fraction of the flower that has nibbles in it, and the fraction that does not.

$$\frac{3}{9}$$ $$\frac{6}{9}$$

with nibbles   no nibbles

Adding fractions 74

Five out of these nine mice are wearing striped T-shirts. Draw stripes on one more T-shirt. Complete the calculation to show the fraction of mice wearing striped T-shirts.

$$\frac{5}{9} + \frac{1}{9} = \frac{6}{9}$$

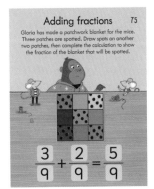

Adding fractions 75

Gloria has made a patchwork blanket for the mice. Three patches are spotted. Draw spots on another two patches, then complete the calculation to show the fraction of the blanket that will be spotted.

$$\frac{3}{9} + \frac{2}{9} = \frac{5}{9}$$

Subtracting fractions 76

Wolfy and Ping have bought a loaf of bread and they are each having two slices of toast. Complete the calculation to show the fraction of the loaf that is left.

$$1 - \frac{4}{9} = \frac{5}{9}$$

whole loaf

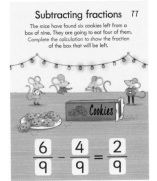

Subtracting fractions 77

The mice have found six cookies left from a box of nine. They are going to eat four of them. Complete the calculation to show the fraction of the box that will be left.

$$\frac{6}{9} - \frac{4}{9} = \frac{2}{9}$$

How many...? 78

This group of friends is at the fair. Fill in the boxes to show the fraction of the group doing each activity.

$$\frac{6}{10}$$ $$\frac{4}{10}$$

tossing rings   doing archery

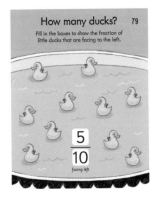

How many ducks? 79

Fill in the boxes to show the fraction of little ducks that are facing to the left.

$$\frac{5}{10}$$

facing left

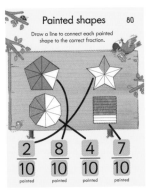

Painted shapes 80

Draw a line to connect each painted shape to the correct fraction.

$$\frac{2}{10}$$ $$\frac{8}{10}$$ $$\frac{4}{10}$$ $$\frac{7}{10}$$

painted   painted   painted   painted

Dividing into tenths 81

Zeb has divided his vegetable patch into tenths. Write the correct fraction inside each part.

$$\frac{1}{10} \quad \frac{1}{10} \quad \frac{1}{10} \quad \frac{1}{10} \quad \frac{1}{10}$$

$$\frac{1}{10} \quad \frac{1}{10} \quad \frac{1}{10} \quad \frac{1}{10} \quad \frac{1}{10}$$

Answers

Equal parts 82

The animals have divided their sponge cakes into ten portions. Circle the cake that is divided into tenths.

What fraction? 83

Look at the flower below. Then, fill in the boxes to show the fraction of the flower that has nibbles in it, and the fraction that does not.

$$\frac{5}{10}$$ with nibbles $$\frac{5}{10}$$ no nibbles

Adding fractions 84

Zeb has painted two tenths of this fence red and Hop has painted four tenths blue. Complete the calculation to show the fraction of the fence that is painted.

$$\frac{2}{10} + \frac{4}{10} = \frac{6}{10}$$

Adding fractions 85

Ping is laying a path with ten slabs. He has laid eight tenths of the path and has two slabs still to lay. Complete the calculation to show the fraction of the path that will be built once they are laid.

$$\frac{8}{10} + \frac{2}{10} = \frac{10}{10}$$ or $$1$$ whole wall

Subtracting fractions 86

Together, Pin, Hop and Pat have three tenths of Bruce's homemade orange tart. Complete the calculation to show the fraction of the tart that is left.

$$1$$ whole tart $$- \frac{3}{10} = \frac{7}{10}$$

Subtracting fractions 87

Zeb and Pin are sharing a pizza. They have eaten six tenths of it so far. Complete the calculation to show the fraction of the pizza that is left.

$$1$$ whole pizza $$- \frac{6}{10} = \frac{4}{10}$$

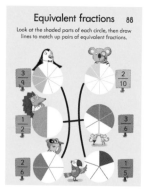

Equivalent fractions 88

Look at the shaded parts of each circle, then lines to match up pairs of equivalent fractions.

Unit fractions 89

A unit fraction is one part of a whole. Circle all the unit fractions below.

Fractions match-up 90

Draw a line from each fraction to its matching cloud.

Answers

Ordering fractions 91

Draw a line to connect all these plates in order. Start with the plate that has the smallest fraction of cake and finish with the largest.

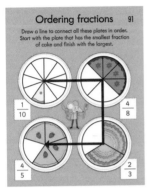

$\frac{1}{10}$ $\frac{4}{8}$

$\frac{4}{5}$ $\frac{2}{3}$

Equivalent fractions 92

Look at the shaded parts of each circle, then draw lines to match up pairs of equivalent fractions.

$\frac{4}{6}$ $\frac{4}{8}$

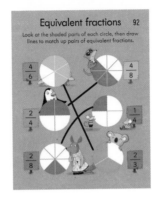

$\frac{2}{4}$ $\frac{1}{4}$

$\frac{2}{8}$ $\frac{2}{3}$

Unit fractions 93

A unit fraction is one part of a whole. Circle all the unit fractions below.

$\frac{7}{10}$ $\frac{1}{8}$ $\frac{3}{5}$

$\frac{4}{4}$ $\frac{5}{7}$ $\frac{1}{5}$

Fractions match-up 94

Draw a line from each fraction to its matching cloud.

$\frac{2}{8}$ four ninths $\frac{3}{6}$

eight tenths

three sixths $\frac{4}{9}$ four sevenths

$\frac{4}{7}$ $\frac{8}{10}$

two eighths

Ordering fractions 95

Draw a line to connect all these plates in order. Start with the plate that has the smallest fraction of pie and finish with the largest.

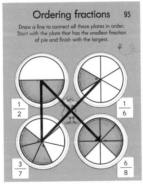

$\frac{1}{2}$ $\frac{1}{6}$

$\frac{3}{7}$ $\frac{6}{8}$

Equivalent fractions 96

Look at the shaded parts of each circle, then draw lines to match up pairs of equivalent fractions.

$\frac{6}{9}$ $\frac{3}{6}$

$\frac{4}{6}$ $\frac{5}{10}$

$\frac{8}{10}$ $\frac{4}{5}$

Equivalent fractions 97

Help the mice match up these balloons. Draw lines to pair them into equivalent fractions.

$\frac{2}{3}$ $\frac{2}{4}$ $\frac{4}{6}$

$\frac{2}{10}$ $\frac{1}{2}$ $\frac{1}{5}$

Ordering fractions 98

Draw a line to connect all these plates in order. Start with the plate that has the smallest fraction of cheese and finish with the largest.

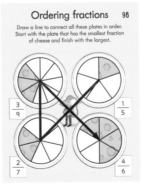

$\frac{3}{9}$ $\frac{1}{5}$

$\frac{2}{7}$ $\frac{4}{6}$

Equivalent fractions 99

Look at the shaded parts of each circle, then draw lines to match up pairs of equivalent fractions.

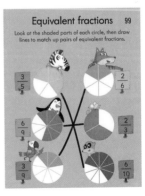

$\frac{3}{5}$ $\frac{2}{6}$

$\frac{6}{9}$ $\frac{2}{3}$

$\frac{3}{9}$ $\frac{6}{10}$

Answers

Equivalent fractions 100

Help the mice match up these kites. Draw lines to pair them into equivalent fractions.

$\frac{5}{10}$ $\frac{7}{7}$ $\frac{1}{4}$

$\frac{2}{8}$ $\frac{9}{9}$ $\frac{3}{6}$

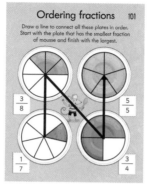

Ordering fractions 101

Draw a line to connect all these plates in order. Start with the plate that has the smallest fraction of mousse and finish with the largest.

$\frac{3}{8}$ $\frac{5}{5}$

$\frac{1}{7}$ $\frac{3}{4}$

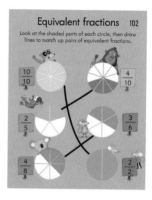

Equivalent fractions 102

Look at the shaded parts of each circle, then draw lines to match up pairs of equivalent fractions.

$\frac{10}{10}$ $\frac{4}{10}$

$\frac{2}{5}$ $\frac{3}{6}$

$\frac{4}{8}$ $\frac{2}{2}$

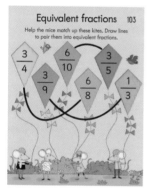

Equivalent fractions 103

Help the mice match up these kites. Draw lines to pair them into equivalent fractions.

$\frac{3}{4}$ $\frac{6}{10}$ $\frac{3}{5}$

$\frac{3}{9}$ $\frac{6}{8}$ $\frac{1}{3}$

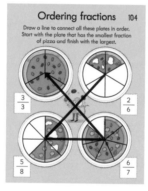

Ordering fractions 104

Draw a line to connect all these plates in order. Start with the plate that has the smallest fraction of pizza and finish with the largest.

$\frac{3}{3}$ $\frac{2}{6}$

$\frac{5}{8}$ $\frac{6}{7}$

Equivalent fractions 105

Help the mice match up these balloons. Draw lines to pair them into equivalent fractions.

$\frac{4}{5}$ $\frac{8}{8}$ $\frac{4}{8}$

$\frac{8}{10}$ $\frac{6}{6}$ $\frac{1}{2}$

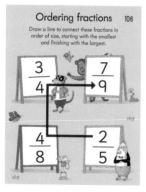

Ordering fractions 106

Draw a line to connect these fractions in order of size, starting with the smallest and finishing with the largest.

$\frac{3}{4}$ $\frac{7}{9}$

$\frac{4}{8}$ $\frac{2}{5}$

Equivalent fractions 107

Help the mice match up these signs. Draw lines to pair them into equivalent fractions.

$\frac{4}{10}$ $\frac{1}{3}$ $\frac{6}{10}$

$\frac{2}{5}$ $\frac{3}{5}$ $\frac{2}{6}$

Ordering fractions 108

Draw a line to connect these fractions in order of size, starting with the smallest and finishing with the largest.

$\frac{1}{2}$ $\frac{2}{8}$

$\frac{5}{6}$ $\frac{10}{10}$

Answers

True or false? 109

Read the statements below, and write a 'T' next to the ones that are true, and an 'F' next to the ones that are false.

$\frac{3}{6}$ is equivalent to $\frac{1}{2}$ **T**

$\frac{4}{8}$ is equivalent to $\frac{3}{5}$ **F**

$\frac{1}{3}$ is equivalent to $\frac{2}{6}$ **T**

$\frac{7}{7}$ is equivalent to $\frac{9}{10}$ **F**

Ordering fractions 110

Draw a line to connect these fractions in order of size, starting with the smallest and finishing with the largest.

$\frac{3}{5}$ $\frac{1}{9}$

$\frac{4}{4}$ $\frac{7}{8}$

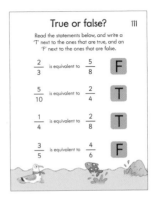

True or false? 111

Read the statements below, and write a 'T' next to the ones that are true, and an 'F' next to the ones that are false.

$\frac{2}{3}$ is equivalent to $\frac{5}{8}$ **F**

$\frac{5}{10}$ is equivalent to $\frac{2}{4}$ **T**

$\frac{1}{4}$ is equivalent to $\frac{2}{8}$ **T**

$\frac{3}{5}$ is equivalent to $\frac{4}{6}$ **F**

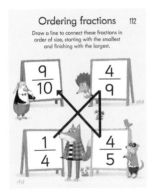

Ordering fractions 112

Draw a line to connect these fractions in order of size, starting with the smallest and finishing with the largest.

$\frac{9}{10}$ $\frac{4}{9}$

$\frac{1}{4}$ $\frac{4}{5}$

True or false? 113

Read the statements below, and write a 'T' next to the ones that are true, and an 'F' next to the ones that are false.

$\frac{2}{10}$ is equivalent to $\frac{1}{5}$ **T**

$\frac{2}{3}$ is equivalent to $\frac{6}{9}$ **T**

$\frac{4}{6}$ is equivalent to $\frac{2}{4}$ **F**

$\frac{1}{4}$ is equivalent to $\frac{4}{8}$ **F**

Ordering fractions 114

Draw a line to connect these fractions in order of size, starting with the smallest and finishing with the largest.

$\frac{4}{6}$ $\frac{1}{3}$

$\frac{2}{10}$ $\frac{7}{7}$

True or false? 115

Read the statements below, and write a 'T' next to the ones that are true, and an 'F' next to the ones that are false.

$\frac{1}{3}$ is equivalent to $\frac{2}{9}$ **F**

$\frac{6}{8}$ is equivalent to $\frac{3}{4}$ **T**

$\frac{6}{9}$ is equivalent to $\frac{3}{3}$ **F**

$\frac{4}{5}$ is equivalent to $\frac{8}{10}$ **T**

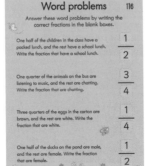

Word problems 116

Answer these word problems by writing the correct fractions in the blank boxes.

One half of the children in the class have a packed lunch, and the rest have a school lunch. Write the fraction that have a school lunch. $\frac{1}{2}$

One quarter of the animals on the bus are listening to music, and the rest are chatting. Write the fraction that are chatting. $\frac{3}{4}$

Three quarters of the eggs in the carton are brown, and the rest are white. Write the fraction that are white. $\frac{1}{4}$

One half of the ducks on the pond are male, and the rest are female. Write the fraction that are female. $\frac{1}{2}$

Halves 117

Write the answers to these questions in the boxes.

$\frac{1}{2}$ of 10 = **5** $\frac{1}{2}$ of 90 = **45**

$\frac{1}{2}$ of 30 = **15** $\frac{1}{2}$ of 26 = **13**

$\frac{1}{2}$ of 48 = **24** $\frac{1}{2}$ of 64 = **32**

What is half of each of these numbers? $\frac{1}{2}$ of 18 = **9**

We'll need to divide each number by two.

Answers

Word problems 118

Answer these word problems by writing the correct fractions in the blank boxes.

One third of the roses in Kat's vase are red, and the rest are white. Write the fraction that are white. $\frac{2}{3}$

Two fifths of the pirates on the ship have beards, and the rest do not. Write the fraction that do not have beards. $\frac{3}{5}$

Four fifths of the candles on Wolfy's birthday cake are lit, and the rest are not. Write the fraction that are not lit. $\frac{1}{5}$

Two thirds of the sheep in the field are lying down, and the rest are standing. Write the fraction that are standing. $\frac{1}{3}$

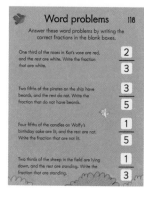

Quarters 119

Write the answers to these questions in the boxes.

$\frac{1}{4}$ of 20 = 5 $\frac{2}{4}$ of 36 = 18

$\frac{2}{4}$ of 14 = 7 $\frac{1}{4}$ of 16 = 4

$\frac{3}{4}$ of 44 = 33 $\frac{3}{4}$ of 8 = 6

First, divide each number by four...

...then you'll know what one quarter of the number is.

$\frac{1}{4}$ of 28 = 7

Word problems 120

Answer these word problems by writing the correct fractions in the blank boxes.

Four tenths of the pins in the bowling lane are standing, and Zeb has knocked the rest down. Write the fraction that have been knocked down. $\frac{6}{10}$

Three eighths of the nuts in Pat's jar are hazelnuts, and the rest are almonds. Write the fraction that are almonds. $\frac{5}{8}$

Eight tenths of the butterflies in the garden are orange, and the rest are purple. Write the fraction of the butterflies that are purple. $\frac{2}{10}$

Two sixths of the animals in the pool are wearing goggles, and the rest are not. Write the fraction that are not wearing goggles. $\frac{4}{6}$

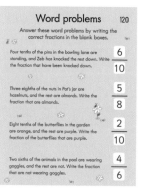

Thirds 121

Write the answers to these questions in the boxes.

$\frac{1}{3}$ of 9 = 3 $\frac{1}{3}$ of 30 = 10

$\frac{1}{3}$ of 27 = 9 $\frac{2}{3}$ of 60 = 40

$\frac{2}{3}$ of 21 = 14 $\frac{2}{3}$ of 12 = 8

First, divide each number by three...

...then you'll know what one third of the number is.

$\frac{1}{3}$ of 18 = 6

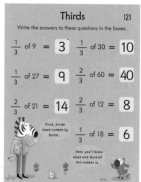

Word problems 122

Answer these word problems by writing the correct fractions in the blank boxes.

Five sevenths of the boats on the lake have sails, and the rest have oars. Write the fraction that have oars. $\frac{2}{7}$

Six ninths of the rabbits in the warren are sleeping. Write the fraction that are awake. $\frac{3}{9}$

Six sevenths of the trees in the park are oak trees, and the rest are beech trees. Write the fraction that are beech trees. $\frac{1}{7}$

Three ninths of the seats on the train are occupied, and the rest are empty. Write the fraction that are empty. $\frac{6}{9}$

Fifths 123

Write the answers to these questions in the boxes.

$\frac{1}{5}$ of 5 = 1 $\frac{3}{5}$ of 40 = 24

$\frac{2}{5}$ of 15 = 6 $\frac{2}{5}$ of 20 = 8

$\frac{4}{5}$ of 35 = 28 $\frac{3}{5}$ of 25 = 15

First, divide each number by five...

...then you'll know what one fifth of the number is.

$\frac{1}{5}$ of 55 = 11

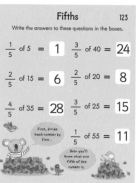

Word problems 124

Answer these word problems by writing the correct numbers in the blank boxes.

There are twenty birds in the tree. Half are singing and the rest are building nests. How many are building nests? 10

There are thirty-five vehicles on the road. Two fifths are trucks, and the rest are cars. How many are cars? 21

There are fourteen cookies in Ping's tin. Four sevenths are milk chocolate, and the rest are dark chocolate. How many are dark chocolate? 6

There are sixty marbles in Bruce's bag. Five tenths are green, and the rest are blue. How many of the marbles are blue? 30

Sixths 125

Write the answers to these questions in the boxes.

$\frac{1}{6}$ of 36 = 6 $\frac{4}{6}$ of 6 = 4

$\frac{3}{6}$ of 18 = 9 $\frac{5}{6}$ of 12 = 10

$\frac{2}{6}$ of 24 = 8 $\frac{1}{6}$ of 42 = 7

First, divide each number by six...

...then you'll know what one sixth of the number is.

$\frac{3}{6}$ of 30 = 15

Word problems 126

Answer these word problems by writing the correct numbers in the blank boxes.

There are eighteen jars on the shelf. Two thirds contain strawberry jam, and the rest contain raspberry. How many contain raspberry jam? 6

There are forty-eight trains in Hop's toy box. Four sixths are red, and the rest are green. How many of the trains are green? 16

There are twenty-seven hikers on the mountain. Six ninths are walking up the mountain, and the rest are walking down. How many are walking down? 9

There are fourteen glasses on the table. Half are filled with juice, and the rest are empty. How many glasses are empty? 7